If I were a ...

dog

Written by Annabel Blackledge
Illustrated by Kate Mullins

PANGOLIN BOOKS

If I were a dog,
I'd have a wet and shiny nose,
a floppy tongue,

a hairy coat
and fur between my toes.

If I were a dog,
I'd chase cats just for fun.

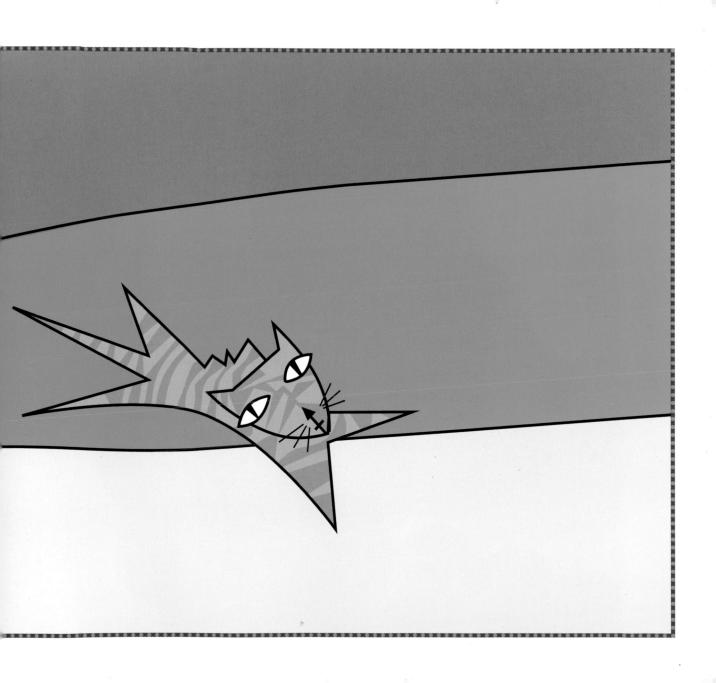

I'd tear around the garden,

then sit

panting

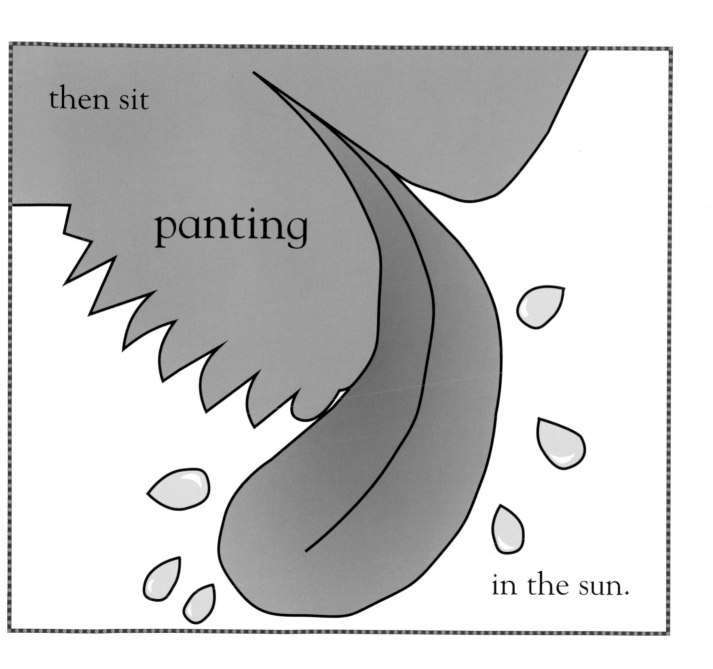

in the sun.

I'd doze
most days ...

and **howl**
most nights ...

and eat my
food up fast.

I'd sit beside the window
to watch the world go past.

I'd take my owner
for a walk –

every single day.

I'd pull my lead and sniff strange smells,

then play and play and play.

I'd fetch big sticks
and other things ...

like leaves,

and then I'd try ...

to jump up with my muddy paws ...

on strangers passing by.

If I were a dog,

I'd be a loving,

faithful

friend.

And everyone I met would
grow to love me in the end.

Published in the UK in 2004 by:

Pangolin Books
Unit 17, Piccadilly Mill, Lower Street,
Stroud, Gloucestershire, GL5 2HT

A CIP catalogue for this book is available
from the British Library.

ISBN 1 84493 017 3

Colour reproduction by
Black Cat Graphics Ltd, Bristol, UK
Printed in the UK by Goodman Baylis Ltd